THE BEARY POSSESSIVE GRIZZLY

Bear Clan, 5

JENIKA SNOW

The BEARy Possessive Grizzly (Bear Clan, 5)

By Jenika Snow

www.JenikaSnow.com

Jenika_Snow@Yahoo.com

Copyright © October 2019 by Jenika Snow

First E-book Publication: October 2019

Cover model: Andrew England

Cover photo provided by: Andrew England

Cover designer: Designs by Dana

Editor: Kayla Robichaux

Cason

I devoted my life to working, building a career and business, making sure I was secure and stable in my life for the sole purpose that I'd find her, that everything would be ready and perfect for *her*.

My mate.

The one woman who would complete me.

The one woman who was born to be mine alone.

Watching my brothers find their other halves hadn't been easy, but I knew I would never give up. I couldn't. My mate would make all the bullshit disappear. She'd make my life have purpose. And that's the only thing that mattered to a bear shifter. To me.

If there was one thing I knew without a doubt, it was that once I found her, I wouldn't go easy.. I would make her see that, once she was mine, that was it. There was no going back.

Mena

Half bear, half human. That's what I was.

My human side dominant. No shifting, no primal urge to be in my animal form. But I was okay with that.

I'd grown up with parents who wanted only the best for me, and that meant not being with a shifter, because of the politics that went along with it, because my father was an outcast for loving my mother—a human who wasn't his fated mate.

Love who you want. That's what they said. That's what they lived by.

But I needed to find myself, needed to find what I wanted out of life. And so I took an impromptu camping trip. I wanted to get away, to reconnect with my bear side, even if she was buried deep down within my human genetics.

But I wasn't alone. He found me, this alpha grizzly bear shifter who looked at me like I was the sun he'd been searching for his entire life.

His mate.

Mine, he growled out like the feral animal he was.

And in that moment, I knew there was no going back.

Prologue

Cason

I stood on my deck, leaning against the railing as I stared off into the forest. The sounds of birds filled my head, and the sight of animals scurrying deep within the woods was something I was able to pick up with my shifter vision. I was shirtless, my sweats hanging low on my hips, wild energy pumping through my veins. I already shifted twice today, let my bear free, let him be wild, but I was ready for round three.

If I were being honest, I was not the type of person who particularly enjoyed being around others. I liked my solitude, my little piece of land away from everyone and everything. I'd built my cabin far away from my brothers—not because I didn't enjoy their company, but because it was just easier for me to be with my own thoughts.

And now that four out of the six of us had found our mates, with only Damon and myself without our other halves, it was a lot fucking easier to be on my own. Seeing my brothers happy and content, their fated mates by their sides, their families growing, had this ache settling deep within me.

So yeah, being alone was really fucking good for me.

As the years passed, and the idea of my female grew further and further away, I realized that being out here was for the best. I'd started becoming grumpier, more animalistic. I let my bear out more than I was sure any other shifter consciously did.

One thing I was sure most humans didn't know, one thing shifters kept tightly guarded, was the fact that the more times we let our animals out, the more times we shifted to let it be free, the more primal we became.

I was right on the verge of just saying fuck it all and being a bear full-time. But I'd miss a lot of shit being human afforded me: enjoying a nice meal, and sitting around the campfire with my brothers and shooting the shit.

I'd miss a lot of fucking things about being a human.

But the truth was, it was easier to be a bear. Less hectic, less confusing. There were no responsibilities or expectations. I lived off the land and just let my basic urges run free. And it was incredible. It was exhilarating and liberating. But whether I was in human form or shifted as a bear, there was one thing that was deeply rooted in me, something that grew by the second.

My mate.

It was this growing feeling inside of me, like this seed was planted deep inside me and every year it grew until one day it would just burst free, tearing me from the inside out.

I had one sole purpose on this planet, and that was to find my mate, to claim her, mark her, to get her swollen with my child. And the very thought, the picture of her big and round, my baby growing inside her, my mark on her neck, was nearly enough to send me into a frenzy of possessive need.

I didn't know where or who she was, but what I did know for certain was that if I ever did find her, I was going to claim her so fucking hard there was no turning back.

I just hoped I wasn't more animal than human when that time came.

Chapter One

Mena

"When are you going to find a nice man, Mena honey?"

I stopped midbite as I looked up at my father. "A nice man?" I asked with a mouthful of my mother's homemade meatloaf.

"Well, a nice human, sweetheart."

I set my fork down and reached for my glass of red wine, taking a long drink from it before I answered. Having a father who was a bear shifter and a mother who was human meant my father was an outcast from the moment he decided to marry and be with someone not his fated mate. But he'd fallen head-over-heels in love with my mother, mate or not, because after forty years of him being alone, he was done looking for that "soulmate." And I couldn't blame him, was glad they'd been happy and found each other.

I'd been their midlife baby, the surprise they thought they'd never be able to have any children. I'd taken after my mother's side, fully human but with slight bear-shifting genetics. My senses were keener, more heightened. And my drive for the wilderness was there, so strong I found myself in the woods weekly just to touch base with nature.

But actually shifting into a bear? Never going to happen for me.

So here I was, my father salty because he was estranged from his bear side, and both my parents wanting nothing more for me than to be happy and live a shifter-free life with a banker husband, a white picket fence around our three-bedroom home, and popping out little human babies.

"We just want you to go after what you deserve, honey." My mother brought her fork to her mouth, the prongs speared with romaine and spinach, a dollop of thick ranch dressing dripping onto her plate.

I glanced at my father, who was in the process of cutting into his pretty much rare steak. The focus he had on the piece of meat was akin to being in love.

"I'm actually going to head to bear country for the week to go camping." That had my father glancing up midchew. Bear country wasn't the town's real name, but it was one the residents and anyone who lived within a hundred-mile radius called it. Mainly because the population of bear shifters in that area and the surrounding parts was pretty thick.

"Bear country?"

I nodded at his question. "Yeah. Isn't any mountain town filled with wild animals?" I asked in confusion.

My father lifted a salt-and-pepper, bushy eyebrow.

"And you're camping? Like in a tent or one of those rent-a-cabins?" There was worry in my mother's voice, and I almost scoffed.

"I'm gonna rough it. Full-on middle of nowhere, pitching a tent, and starting a fire all by myself."

My mom and dad glanced worriedly at each other.

"You think that's a good idea? Safe? The bear shifters that live in the forest are feral, Mena. They aren't like the bears who live in towns. They are in their animal form more than they are human."

I did roll my eyes then and scoffed. "I don't even know if there will be bear shifters where I'll be. And if there are, I'm sure I'll be fine. It's not like I'm not bringing protection.

"Protection?" My mother all but gasped that word and quickly covered her mouth with her hand. She leaned in closer. "Like a gun?" she whispered.

"Oh my God, Mom." I couldn't help but laugh. "Firstly, you make it sound like a dirty word. Secondly, no, I am not bringing a gun. I don't even own one."

"Oh, thank fuck."

"Harold," my mother hissed and glanced at my dad. "You know I don't like that kind of language."

"Sorry, dear."

"I have pepper spray and my hunting knife Dad gave me for my fifteenth birthday. I'll be fine. Promise." I smiled. "Dad taught me all I need to know to survive out in the woods." I glanced at my father and he grinned, his chest puffing out in pride.

"Damn right I did."

My mother, being human, was against all forms of violence. But having a bear shifter for a father meant I learned all about surviving in the woods and how to take care of myself.

"Are you taking any of your friends, honey?" My mom went back to eating her dinner, but her focus was on me.

I shook my head. "No. This trip is just for me. With work and finals, I'm pretty stressed. So when I take my last exam, I'm going to have my car packed for the week and just head out." I could see the pride in my father's face, but also the worry.

He may have taught me how to survive, but that didn't mean he also hadn't told me about all the strangers.

He was nervous, probably more so than my mother. He knew all about how bear shifters could be. Because he'd been an outcast for falling in love with a human female who wasn't his mate, he'd seen the ugly side of his kind.

But no matter what, he still didn't try to hide who and what he was. Who and what a part of me was.

* * *

IT WAS twenty minutes later when we finished eating, and as I helped my mom clean up, my dad called me into the other room. I headed into his study and saw him sitting by his desk. Being a high school English teacher meant he did a lot of work from home, grading papers, doing lesson plans. The end of the school day wasn't the end of the day for him.

So when he opened up his drawer and pulled out a gun case—*the* gun case—I felt my eyes widen a little.

He unzipped the case and opened the top, turning it around so I could see his pistol. I knew it had been in his family for a very long time, something that had been passed down to the men in his family. His father had given it to him before he was shunned from his clan.

I looked between the gun and him and back again. "Dad, what is this?" Of course I knew what it was. I just wasn't sure why he was showing it to me.

"I want you to have this."

Surely he didn't think I was so helpless I would need it for my short-term camping trip.

"Listen, I want you to be safe and protected, and sometimes a hunting knife just doesn't do the trick."

I was shaking my head before he finished. "Dad,

it's legit like a week I'll be gone. I'm not going to the middle of nowhere. The town is like twenty minutes away."

He chuckled in that deep, husky voice I was familiar with. "This isn't just for the camping trip. I've wanted to give you this for some time. I figure now is as good a time as any." He smiled. "You're my little girl still, even if you're all grown up. And I want to make sure you know how to handle yourself." He leaned in and kissed the top of my head, and I smiled. "Be safe, but most of all be content and happy. Know what you want in life and follow through with it all the way."

He ruffled my hair before turning and leaving me. I looked down at the gun sitting in the case and ran my fingers over the cold metal. I was glad I had supportive parents who accepted anything and everything I decided to do with my life.

Now, I just needed to realize what I actually wanted to do.

Chapter Two

Mena

I took a step back and cursed as I felt sweat start to form on my forehead from pitching the tent. I placed my hands on my hips, staring at the small two-person tent currently situated between a couple large pine trees.

I turned and went back to my car and pulled out the padded mats, setting them inside the tent, and then made a couple more trips to grab my sleeping bag, some blankets, and all the other camping paraphernalia I needed.

I hadn't been camping in forever, but damn could I still make one good-ass campsite.

I popped the trunk and looked at the four boxes

of food and five jugs of water my mother and father packed, and all I could do was smile and shake my head. I was only going to be gone for about a week, yet they'd given me enough stuff it was like I would be gone for a month.

When I looked down at my cell, I saw I had zero bars of service. But instead of worrying about that, I felt a sense of relief.

It was another fifteen minutes of getting everything situated before I finally sat down to start making a fire. Once the flames were licking across the wood, the sound of crackling filling my head, the smell of smoke mixing with the scent of evergreens and pine trees, I felt calmness settle in.

Despite my human side being dominant, my bear did come out when I was surrounded by nature. Being in the woods made my animal side content and relaxed.

It made me happy.

It made me feel like I was at home.

Cason

I STOOD AT THE LEDGE, looking down over the sleepy, quiet town below. This was my home, the place I called mine my entire life. The construction business with my brothers, my side business of woodworking... my life was pretty damn near perfect.

But then again, it wasn't.

I felt like I was missing a part of myself, an integral piece that would make me whole, make me complete.

And that was my mate.

Six brothers, four of them having found their fated females, yet here I was—myself and Damon—mateless, missing a part of ourselves. And the truth was, we may never find our females. It wasn't unheard of. In fact, there were plenty of instances where shifters had given up hope of finding their other halves. And so they fell in love with humans or other shifters. They had families. They started lives with them. And although that was an option, the truth was I didn't want that. I'd rather be alone than be with a female who wasn't fully mine, wasn't born to be solely my mate.

Closing my eyes and just inhaling and exhaling slowly, I felt my bear stir, felt him rise up from deep within me and push forward for supremacy. I'd been letting him out more and more, my human starting to feel more submissive as my animal became dominant. Although he'd always been at the forefront, it was my human side who took precedence. But not lately.

I was starting to feel more animal than human, and that was a dangerous situation. Because when a shifter let his animal side reign supreme, it was hard going back. It was hard not to just be in animal form full-time, letting yourself be one with nature, not letting any of the bullshit of the human world consume you.

I started taking off my clothes, enjoying being out here in the middle of nowhere, only nature surrounding me. The property myself and my brothers owned was vast and extensive.

When I had my shirt and pants off, the material pooled by my feet. I was about to remove my briefs when the scent of burning wood from a fire filled my nostrils.

I growled low. This was our property, and anyone on it was trespassing. I could picture young college assholes pitching tents and starting camp-fires, drinking beer and smoking pot. My animal was dying to come forward, my bones and muscles pushing out of my skin, my body all but shifting, changing for the impending transformation. And I let it overtake me.

I let it rip through my human form until I was on all fours now, my claws digging into the dirt.

I started making my way toward where the fire was coming from, the scent of burning wood growing more potent. The closer I got, the more I heard the crackling of the flames moving over the logs, eating at it until there would be nothing left.

The scent of smoke was strong, masking any other I could pick up. And when I was finally at the campsite a few yards away, hidden behind the woods, watching, taking everything in, I was surprised to see only one vehicle. I didn't even see anyone, but the tent door was open, and the sound of rustling within it was loud.

"Shit."

The sound of the feminine voice cursing had my ears picking up. I felt my body tighten even further. All anger left me. Curiosity grew. The feeling of something monumental piqued my interest.

I stood a little bit taller, a little bit straighter outside that tent. There was something about her voice, something that pulled at me. It was just a feeling that had my bear becoming restless. I was having a hard time controlling him, the bastard starting to pace back and forth, his nails digging into the ground, this low growl leaving him. I was confused, didn't know what was going on. The only thing I knew was I didn't want to relent, didn't want to turn around and leave, to stop the sound of that voice from penetrating me and seeping into every single cell in my body.

I found myself taking a step closer, moving toward that campsite almost as if my life depended on it. It was this tether inside me, pulling me forward. And it was only when I was several feet from the campsite that I finally stopped, my human side becoming a little bit stronger.

I took in the scene, trying to figure out what was going on and why I was acting like this. And then I saw her emerge from the tent, the fall of her long dark hair coming out of the haphazard ponytail she had at the top of her head.

My heart stopped, seized in my chest. The air left me, my body tightening, and everything in me came alive, awake. It was this feeling of my muscles contracting and relaxing. It was the sensation of being... home.

My mate.

My mate stood right in front of me, and she didn't even know what she was about to get herself into, what type of possessive beast she'd been mated to.

Chapter Three

Mena

I heard a snap of a twig close by and tipped my head back to look out in the woods. The sun was just starting to set, colors of orange and pink painting the horizon as it washed over the forest and the campsite. It gave it this hazy, almost romantic feel, a cotton candy sense of wonder that made it seem like I was somewhere else, living in another world.

I turned around and scanned my surroundings, the knife my father had given me already in my hand. The sound of the fire crackling and the scent of wood burning filled my senses. I was getting supper ready, and although I wasn't afraid, didn't feel any kind of worry because of nature and the sound it created, that it made me feel, I was observant and on guard, ready if need be.

I inhaled deeply, since my sense of smell was normally acute and precise, but the fire masked many things. There was no wind, no presence of a breeze that would give me the scent of what was nearby.

As I looked into the woods, the darkness started to creep forward, to come in closer toward me, obscuring the trees, hiding them in the shadow of a blanket. I felt myself relax. There were animals of all kinds in these woods, big and small, just as afraid of me as I would be of them.

I loosened the grip on my knife and sat back down on the fallen log that happened to be in position parallel with the fire. With my back to my tent, I stared at those flames. I was content and happy, right in my element. I reached for the little pot and grate that would make up my stove and placed it over the flames.

I opened up the cooler and pushed the ice around. The fresh, cold items would only last me a few days before the ice melted, but I had enough prepackaged, non-perishable items to last me the rest of the week. I didn't want to have to keep going back-and-forth into town, and although it was only a twenty minute or so ride, the point of coming out here was to get away from everyone, away from civilization and the crush of being social.

Besides, I'd always been a peanut butter and jelly kind of girl, a protein bar and fresh fruit kind of hiker. I could handle this, could deal with it even if I had to eat beef jerky out of a bag for the next seven days.

The wind started picking up then, coming from up north, down the mountain. It washed away the scent of smoke and fire, and I inhaled deeply once more, finally smelling the forest in front of me. Squirrels and rabbits, even a wolf in the distance. But there was a musky aroma, a scent of an animal that was stronger, more powerful.

A bear.

As I took in that scent once more, something in me shifted, my inner animal slowly rising, trying to wade through my human side. She was trying to get out.

Although I felt my bear's strength throughout the years, I'd never felt the kind of push she was giving right now. It's like she was attempting to fight for supremacy, like she wanted to break free and be the dominant one. And it was a new, frightening but exciting feeling. The very thought of shifting, of letting her take control, actually being in my bear form for once in my life, gave me this excited and anxious feeling.

I stood then, the blade in my palm, my fingers wrapped tightly around the handle, and I glanced into the woods where the scent and noise came from. The bear was still there, powerful and strong, saturating the air. It was a male. A grizzly.

I closed my eyes and breathed in deeply through my nose. Wild. Musky. Alpha. But there was some other scent mixed with all of that, one I couldn't place, couldn't decipher what it meant.

But what I did know was that it made me feel like I wanted more... made me want one thing.

Him.

Chapter Four

Cason

I didn't go any closer her— even though I desperately wanted to, and even though I wanted to make my presence known and tell her she was mine.

Instead, I waited in the darkness, in the shadows. I watched her to make sure she stayed safe, protected. I was going through every scenario in my mind on how I would make her mine.

Charging forwarded in my bear form, roaring out that she was my mate, would most definitely frighten her, would have her running in the other direction from me forever. And that's not what I wanted. I wanted her irrevocably.

For the first time in my life, I felt like I'd actually found where I was supposed to be, found what had always been mine. My life had meaning now, purpose. It was like all the other bullshit I'd done thus far had just been preparing me for this one moment, this one time where I would lay eyes on what was mine, on who was born to be by my side.

My mate, my wife, and the mother of my children—that's what she was to me.

My everything.

I watched as she sat by the fire, staring into the flames. There was a little bowl in her lap filled with some peaches she'd poured out of a can. God, she was gorgeous with the wisps of her hair falling out from her ponytail. All kinds of possessive, filthy things ran through my head, things that had me envisioning pulling on those strands and tilting her head back as I stared at the arch of her neck, as I bared it to me and marked her.

My mouth salivated to do just that, my canines aching to pierce the tender flesh of her skin and create the mark that would let all others know she was mine, that she was forever taken.

I took a step closer to her, a twig snapping under my paw. But she didn't look up. She knew I was still here. As I inhaled deeply and took in the scent of her human side, I also smelled the bear inside her trying to come out.

She was half shifter, yet her human genetics were dominant. Her bear was being drowned, submerged by her human DNA. It stopped her from shifting. I could smell she'd never done it, never experienced that pleasure of letting your bear out and having it run free.

But I knew that would change once I mated with her. I knew once my mark was on her, she'd feel her animal rise up, ripping, clawing from the dark depths within her. She'd shift. Not just for herself, but for me. She'd give me the pleasure, the privilege of seeing her animal finally break free, finally experience the joys of being able to run in the woods, feel the air, the wind move across her fur.

And every thought made me harder, more aroused. It made me want to just go over to her right now and take her.

"I know you're out there," she called as she stared at the fire, spearing a peach with the prongs of her fork and bringing it to her mouth.

I watched some of that peach juice slip down her full bottom lip, and a low growl of arousal and approval left me.

"I know you're a shifter, so you might as well come out and stop hiding." She lifted her head and looked in my direction then, and although it was pitch black, and even though she was only half-shifter, I knew she could see me watching her. "I didn't come here to be watched and stalked while I'm on vacation."

I found myself moving closer, unable to stop myself from going to what was mine. When I broke through the tree line, she slowly stood and set her bowl down. I didn't miss the gun she had in her hand. She'd gone into the tent an hour before, rustled around, and had come back out empty-handed. She must have been hiding the weapon. I couldn't blame her though. I wanted her to be safe, to feel safe.

I didn't like that she was out here all alone for God knew how long. It wasn't safe in the woods, and even though this was property that belonged to my family—belonged to her, because she was my mate—that didn't mean it was safe. The elements, the wild animals. She could get hurt, lost.

And when I finally stepped into the clearing, staring at her, watching as her throat worked when she swallowed, smelling her nerves, her anxiousness, I hated that I was the reason she felt this way. I lowered my gaze to her hand, where she held the gun. Her fingers were wrapped tightly around the butt, her hand slightly shaking. She was trying to appear strong, and although she was nervous, she wasn't afraid in the face of clear danger.

Although I wasn't dangerous to her per se, she didn't really know that. Maybe she didn't know I was her mate. Maybe she didn't know we belonged together irrevocably.

She was half-bear, so in hindsight, those kinds of instincts could've been dulled, muted. But the way she looked at me and the scent of her curiosity had this need telling me she felt something more. It might not be as ingrained in her as what I felt, this undeniable bond and irrefutable love I felt for her.

But she would.

I would never walk away from her, no matter what.

Chapter Five

Mena

In front of me stood a massive eight-foot grizzly, his fur dark-brown, almost black in color. His body was powerful. I could smell the Alpha come from him. The realization he wasn't just an animal but a shifter who no doubt lived in these woods made me... warm. I held the gun tightly in my hand, knowing I wouldn't actually use it but having it for show, as well as letting him know if it came down to it I would protect myself at all costs.

"Why don't you shift back? I assume you have something to say to me, because that's surely why you've been lurking in the woods by my campsite this whole time." I was trying not to show him how anxious I was, that his massive size and presence put me on edge. But even so, I didn't feel like he would hurt me. I didn't feel any kind of anxiety that I was in danger.

In fact, I felt the opposite. I felt safe around him, as if anything that tried to harm me, he would come up against as my massive protector. And that was a strange thought given the fact that I didn't know who this person was, who the shifter really was beneath the fur and the power and the height and weight of his bear.

He didn't move for long moments, and I didn't even think he breathed. But then he finally let out of huff, air blowing out his nose as if he were sighing, maybe nervous himself.

I felt the air change, become thicker, hotter. I felt electricity move over me, causing the hair on my arms to stand on end. I watched as his body morphed, shifted from a powerful grizzly bear to the man who stood in front of me. He was still big and massive, his human height close to six and a half feet. He had muscles stacked on each other, and his skin was covered in tattoos. So much ink that I actually felt this tightness pool in my belly. Never had I felt such desire. Never had I thought a man covered in tattoos would be so incredibly sexy.

In fact, I never thought any man was remotely attractive, had never had any desire. And although it was a little strange if I really thought about it, a twenty-something-year-old virgin who had never wanted a relationship, it had never really bothered me, because it had felt right to be alone.

But I looked at this man and all I felt was desire, arousal, and so much need I couldn't breathe.

What was it about him that made me feel this way?

I refused to lower my gaze down to the intimate part of him, but it was hard. It was really damn hard.

And then despite myself saying I wouldn't, I looked down, felt my throat tighten, my eyes widen. There he stood in all his naked glory, hard muscles packed upon each other, tattoos trailing along his abdomen, down his hips, and over his thighs. There was so much ink, more tattoo than his tanned skin.

I felt my body heat, my face blush. My nipples hardened, pressing against the material of my shirt. And my pussy... God, I was getting so wet. And his dick—his dick was massive and long... as thick as my wrist.

My mouth dried.

He was starting to get hard, and I felt my eyes widen even more. This was obscene, me staring at him, him getting aroused. And still I couldn't look away.

I lifted my gaze back up, trying to keep my cool, like there wasn't some naked shifter standing right in front of me getting a hard-on. I blinked a few times and snapped back to reality, looked behind me at my tent, and started walking backward until I could reach down and grab a blanket. I tossed it to him, and when he caught it effortlessly, not saying anything as he wrapped it around his waist, I breathed out slowly. The material was tented in front from his growing erection, and I could see his brow lift at me in maybe curiosity, or almost a challenge.

I gathered my resolve, pushing everything away. The fact that he was gorgeous and naked made me want to go to him and throw myself against his body. I was acting insane, my bear pacing inside me, wanting out for the first time in her life.

"Why are you hiding in the forest just watching

me?" I had to give myself credit. I thought I was handling my shit pretty damn well, not freaking out, even though I wanted to. He said nothing, didn't respond, didn't even move. I watched as his massive chest moved up and down slightly as he breathed, his focus trained right on me.

I lifted up the gun to show him, even though I knew I wouldn't use it, and he probably did as well. "This is fully loaded and I'm not afraid to use it if need be. So why don't you tell me what you want, why you're lurking in the woods like a fucking creep, and then we can both be on our way." My voice was hard and even. I should've won an Emmy for how brave I was acting.

I saw the way the corner of his mouth kicked up in a smirk, and despite how I was acting all collected and calm, my emotions gave me away. He inhaled deeply, this slow sound leaving him. I was afraid—not of him or that he would hurt me, but of this unusual situation. It wasn't that I was a sheltered little girl, but then again, I'd never been up against a massive grizzly shifter before, not counting my father.

I was out of my element and nervous of the situation. And my default setting was to act tough even though I really wasn't.

"You have some fire in your veins, don't you?" His voice was deep and husky and sent an unusual feeling throughout every single part of my body. "I like it." He took a step closer. "My bear fucking loves it."

God. What was happening right now?

My heart started racing even faster, beads of sweat pooling along the length of my spine, between my breasts. I felt those droplets on my temple, as if I'd run a marathon and was trying to catch my breath. What was it about this shifter? I asked myself that over and over again.

I couldn't place it, but it felt... right. And my bear—my animal—she kept pacing, crying out for more. She wanted to escape me. I'd never felt this kind of power from her before. It was exhilarating, exciting, liberating.

"You didn't answer my question." I licked my lips, my voice a little tight.

He cleared his throat and went to lift his hand to rub the back of his neck, as if he were a little bit sheepish over the fact that he'd been caught and called out for creeping on me. I didn't know why I found that endearing.

"I didn't mean to be a fucking creep." He dropped his arm to the side, his other hand still wrapped tightly around the blanket, covering himself, covering the massive erection he still sported.

It took a hell of a lot of self-control not to stare at it, trying not to notice how he tented the material of the blanket.

"I'm on vacation. I don't know what you want...." My voice was nothing more than a whisper, because the truth was, I didn't want him to go, and I didn't know why that was.

"This property is owned by myself and my brothers." He didn't say those words as an accusation, not as a judgment, just a fact.

"I—I didn't know. I didn't know this was private property." And I hadn't, hadn't seen any signs posted, didn't even think about it. I felt like a fucking idiot now, my cheeks heating in embarrassment. "I'll leave." That was the first thing I thought of, the only thing I could say now. Here I was giving him shit for hiding in the woods, yet this was his property and I was the one trespassing.

"I don't want you to leave." His words had me freezing, had my eyebrows lifting up in shock.

"But you said it was private property. I'm trespassing." Truth be told, I didn't want to leave either.

We didn't speak for several long seconds, just stared at each other. I wondered what he was thinking. Did he wonder the same, questioning what was going through my mind? Did he feel the same way I did?

I inhaled deeply and could smell his arousal, his desire for me. But there was something else deep down, something that was overpowering, that had taken control even more than his lust was.

And that was possessiveness.

Toward me.

He took a step forward and I took one back. I didn't know I was retreating. There was a different kind of fear settling in me. It had this feeling of the future, of all kinds of possibilities, of how far things would go, filling me.

But still, he kept coming closer, almost stalking me, his head slightly lowered, his eyes trained on me. I took one more step back, my foot catching something on the ground, my body propelling backward as I fell. A startled cry left me, and just as I expected to feel the hard ground greet me, he was right in front of me, his big, strong arms wrapped around my waist, stopping me from falling, pulling me toward his wide, expansive chest.

I dropped my gaze and surprise filled me as I noticed I had my palms flat on his chest, instinctively placed on his pectoral muscles to steady myself.

It felt good to touch him.

His skin was warm, hotter than what I thought it would be. Maybe because he had just shifted from his bear form.

I had to tilt my head back to look into his face, his focus still trained on me, his pupils dilated so much they almost ate up his blue irises. I felt myself fall even deeper, even harder for him.

"I don't know what's going on," I whispered more to myself than to him. I didn't know why I was saying this stuff, having this verbal regurgitation, this messy commentary. It's not like I wanted to say anything at all, because I was confused as hell.

My bear was so powerful right now, stronger than she'd ever been in my entire life. It felt right in his arms. And as she clawed forward, upward, I felt the hair on my arms stand on end, felt my muscles tighten for a moment.

I thought maybe I would actually shift.

But that was impossible. I was too much of a human.

I blinked a few times, reality and common sense slamming into me. I let go of his chest and took a step back, although everything inside of me screamed that I needed to be pressed right to him.

"Maybe I should just go?" Honestly, I was asking myself more than I was him. But he slowly shook his head.

"I told you I don't want you to go."

I took a step back and he followed me one forward. The tent now stopped me from retreating any farther, and I reached out and grabbed the bar that held the structure in place and kept its form.

"I don't know what's happening here." Those words were nothing more than a whisper, meant to stay in my head, but they spilled out, moving between us. I knew he could hear them clear as day despite them being nearly inaudible.

He let this slow growl out and took one more step forward, crowding me. But I liked it. I yearned for more.

"Do you want me to tell you what's going on, little bear?" The way he said that endearment had everything in me clinching, had the most intimate part of me softening... getting wet. He closed his eyes and I saw his nostrils flare slightly as he inhaled deeply. "Do you?"

I licked my lips and I swore I could taste him, this masculine, woodsy, and potent flavor that came from him like a shot of liquor straight to my veins. "Yes." I all but moaned that word and felt my cheeks heat, humiliation flooding me. I'd never acted so out of character before.

"What's your name?"

His voice had my pussy clenching. I was so wet, my panties soaked. I licked my lips again, my mouth so dry, my tongue feeling so thick I didn't even know if I could answer. "Mena," I whispered slightly, wondering if he heard me.

When he opened his eyes, they were completely black, the pupils swallowing up the blue and whiteness. He looked very primal right now, nearly ready to shift again, to show me how powerful his bear really was. And my inner animal was right at the surface, closer to escaping than she'd ever been in my entire life.

"Mena," he said, and it rolled off his tongue almost seductively, as if he drew pleasure from the act. "I'm Cason."

I played his name around in my head over and over again, and it felt so good. It felt so fucking right.

My hands were shaking, my nails feeling like

they were getting longer, turning into claws. "Oh. God."

"No, little bear." He leaned an inch closer, and I swore a piece of paper couldn't have fit between our lips. "Not God. What you've found is your mate."

Chapter Six

Cason

I looked over my shoulder at where she stood in my living room, her eyes bigger as she looked around. The fact that she was actually standing in my home was surreal to me. When I told her she was my mate, I expected shock, maybe even fear. I didn't know much about her, didn't even know if she fully knew her shifter side.

I'd smelled her surprise at how close her bear was to the surface.

She looked at me, this realization, this feeling coming from her and slamming into me. I knew one thing for certain. She accepted it. And so I had given her an ultimatum.

She could stay and camp, and I would stay nearby to watch over, to protect her, because there was no way I was fucking leaving her alone. Or, she could come back to my cabin just a few miles away and we could get to know each other, to figure this out together.

This was new to me just as it was to her. And what shocked the fuck out of me was that she agreed to come home with me. She didn't know who I was, didn't know anything about me, but her heart and soul, her animal, knew she belonged to me as I belonged to her. It was ingrained in us, this undeniable proof that would never go away. We would be linked, connected for the rest of our lives, until we took our last breath.

"Are you thirsty, hungry?" I turned to face her, watching as she seemed a little awestruck at her surroundings. I'd feed her from my hand, make her whatever she wanted. I'd make sure she was full, sated. I wanted that desperately.

So we walked back to my cabin, and then I'd driven her back so we could pack up her camping gear, and now here we were. In any other situation, this probably would have sent red flags up for her, especially in the human world, but with fated mates, it was different. She might be half-human, but she knew me and I knew her. It was this integral feeling we had, this pull and security we both felt. She knew I'd never hurt her. I could see that in her face as she looked at me. I could smell her ease around me.

"I am a little thirsty, if you have any water."

I stared at her a moment, at the arch of her throat as she tipped her head back to look at the ceiling beams and loft. I felt my bear fighting for supremacy, felt my canines elongated, saliva filling my mouth. My nails turned into claws, my body slightly bigger with my impending transformation. And although this wasn't unusual, given the fact that I was starting to become more animal than human, more feral and primal, the reason I was like this right now was because my mate stood just feet from me, in my home, surrounded by my things, by my scent.

I kept picturing tearing off her clothes in a frenzy of passion, tattered remains of material laying across the ground as I lifted her small frame up, my hands cupping her ass, and walked us over to the breakfast counter. I'd set her on it and spread her thighs, step between them. I could practically smell how aroused she'd be, how sweet and musky she'd be for me. All me.

I grabbed her a glass of water, threw a couple cubes of ice in there, and then walked back toward her. She seemed startled when I was right beside her, and the territorial side of me rose up. The way she smiled at me as she tilted her head back and looked at me, the way her fingers brushed against my knuckles when she took the glass... had everything in me lighting up.

It was that small touch that had my eyes flashing. And I knew she saw by the way I scented her surprise, her... arousal.

"Thank you," she said softly. "Your house is so beautiful."

Pleasure filled me at her approval.

"Did you have it custom built?" She went back to looking around.

"I built it. With my brothers' help."

She looked over at me with wide eyes. "Really?" There was wonder in her voice. "You're like..." She glanced around again. "Like a master carpenter."

"It's what I've been doing my whole life. It's a passion of mine. It was my priority." I swallowed roughly. "It was... until you." I stared into her eyes, wanting nothing more than to kiss her.

Her bear was right there, the scent arousing, overpowering, and making me so fucking on edge with need. I could tell that was unusual for her, new.

But by the time I was done with her, by the time she was mine, her bear would be running right beside me, wild and feral... mated.

Chapter Seven

Mena

I had to be insane to just agree to come to some strange man's house, who I met just a couple hours before in the middle of the woods. But I was his mate. He said so. I felt it.

And it made complete sense, as if everything that happened in my life thus far had been leading up to this one moment.

I'd been here for like an hour, sitting on the plush leather couch in front of the fireplace. One thing I noticed about his incredible cabin was that there was no TV, no stereo system. I didn't really notice any appliances on the kitchen counters either. Of course he had a refrigerator, stove, all the main things, but there was no coffee maker, no blender. A man, especially a bachelor, should at least have a television, right?

Instead, he had this ornate fireplace right in front of the living room, with stone detailing and a wood carving of a bear and forest scene on the mantle. It was beautiful and incredible, and the detail was immaculate. You could tell whoever made it had really taken their time, had really loved the work they did.

I looked at Cason and knew he built it, that he'd been the one to put so much passion and love into everything in this home.

I looked back and stared at it for a full minute. But I felt him watching me, his gaze intense. I glanced over at Cason and saw him doing just that, his stare trained on me as he sat in the oversized chair beside me, as if he couldn't take his look off me.

I felt that truth.

I could smell him, the need he had for me, the fact that this was truly my mate, that there was no going back.

I ran that truth through my mind over and over again, loving how it felt, sounded.

Cason.

I said his name repeatedly in my head, loving how it made me feel.

"You must have questions," he finally said in this deep, possessive voice.

I brought the glass to my mouth, the water cold and refreshing against my tongue, down my throat. Oh, I had a shit-load of questions, but none of them sounded realistic; none of them sounded like they made any sense.

"Mates?" I murmured that one word as a question, but of course I knew this was real. My bear was still right below the surface, pacing. Although she wasn't afraid, wasn't as anxious, she was feral in this moment as she tried to get out. She refused to question this.

She accepted this.

And so did I.

"Yes. My mate. Fated mates, Mena." He leaned forward and rested his forearms on his thighs, his big, strong hands clasped together. His biceps were massive, causing me to feel extremely feminine. And his fingers, those digits covered with callouses from doing manual labor and woodworking, nearly made me drool thinking of what they would feel like on my flesh.

"I don't know anything about mates. I'm only

half shifter, never even let my animal out, because she's so dormant." But as I said that last part, I felt my bear push for dominance. She was stronger than my human now. So much stronger.

Those words came for me as if I'd been holding back, as if I couldn't help but speak the truth, telling him everything about me, because it felt so natural. I was so far out of my element; I had no idea what the hell I was doing.

I didn't feel like myself. I was on edge, excited, anxious, ready for the next step in my life.

"Tell me about yourself," he prompted in his deep voice, a sound that had my nerve endings coming alive, lighting on fire.

I set my glass down and rubbed my palms up and down my thighs. My father would kill me if he knew I'd gone home with a stranger. My mother would freak out with worry. But how would they feel if they knew he was my mate?

Although they'd always been hesitant about me being with a shifter because of my father's history, because of how severe and disheartening the shifter community had been to him, I knew in my heart that wasn't how it was with every clan or pack. My father had an unfortunate experience, but I had a supportive family. And although they had their reservations about me being with a non-human, I knew they loved me and respected my decisions in life.

I knew they would be understanding no matter what. "I'm a half-bear shifter, although I know you're already aware of that."

He didn't say anything in response, just nodded slowly, his intense focus still trained on me.

I swallowed roughly again, the lump in my throat refusing to go down.

"You've never shifted." He didn't phrase that like a question, but I nodded anyway.

I was so nervous, my hands shaking so frantically I had to place them under my thighs, trying to calm down, to sit still… attempting to relax my racing heart. The way he stared at me, watched me, made me feel like his prey, like he was the predator. But I'd never wanted to get caught, never wanted to be devoured more than I did with Cason.

For the next ten minutes, I found myself telling him everything about me. I told him about my father being an outcast for loving my mother, who also happened to be his non-mate and a human. I told him I worked part-time at the local real estate office, that I was going to school for business management the other half of the time.

I told him anything and everything, this verbal regurgitation of all the things I felt he should know, of all the things I wanted him to know about me.

He was silent for long moments, but the amount of focus he had on me told me he'd listened— absorbed every single word I said. "What about you?" I whispered, not sure why I was still so nervous.

I've never wanted something—someone—as much as I want him.

"I could listen to you all day… for the rest of my life."

Oh. God.

His words were like accelerant on my already growing emotional fire.

"I want to know about you, though."

He gave me this soft, warm smile, as if that pleased him immensely. "This land is owned by myself and my five brothers, but our cabins are spread out amongst the hundred acres."

There were five other males just like him?

He told me about his woodworking passion, the fact that he worked construction with his brothers on a family owned company. I felt like I was learning the secrets of the world right now, and although this was all new information, it seemed like I'd always known it, like it had been buried deep inside me just waiting to be released.

And when we'd told each other every little bit of detail about us, we sat there just staring at each other.

"I've never shifted before," I blurted out, confirming his words from earlier, the one thing I had never said to anyone besides my parents.

"You will," he said with confidence.

"How do you know?" I asked like it was something he'd know and be able to answer without a doubt.

"Because I can smell the shift nearing in you. You've found me, mate, and that's what your bear was waiting for. She was waiting for her other half to awaken her fully."

His words seemed so… right and perfect.

"This is fast," I whispered, unable to stop the words from spilling from me. "This is insane." But it had never felt so right.

He didn't say anything, just stared at me, as if he knew all the secrets of the world in this very moment. And the weird thing was, even though I felt so out of my depth, so out of my element… I felt like I knew those secrets too.

And then he stood, his big body seeming to take

up my entire view, to fill the entire room. He walked over to me, and I held my breath as I tipped my head back and stared into his face.

"It's all so right." The way he spoke was almost as if he meant to keep it to himself, as if he hadn't wanted me to hear it.

Before I knew what was going on, Cason was right in front of me, his hands on the couch cushions on either side of my body.

"I don't know what's going on," I whispered once again, staring into his blue eyes, my heart beating so fast I felt it in my throat, heard it in my ears. He was on his haunches right between my legs, his hands on my thighs now, the masculinity and power from that small touch sending fireworks through my body.

"You want to know what's going on?" Although he phrased it like a question, I got the feeling he already knew my answer. "What's going on is we've finally found each other, Mena." His voice was this serrated sound, half-human, half-bear.

I could see how tense he was, how much he was fighting the urge to shift into his animal. I felt right on edge with him, so out of control that the only thing that made sense was being with him.

"You don't think this is fast and absolutely

insane?" I knew his answer before he even responded.

He shook his head slowly. "Do you want to stop? Do you want me to take you home, to forget this ever happened?"

I was shaking my head before he finished speaking. "No. That seems so—"

"Wrong?" He finished my sentence, and I nodded.

God, it felt so wrong to be away from him.

"But we don't know each other."

He leaned in close so I felt the warmth of his breath along my lips. "I've known you my entire life, Mena. I may not have known your name or what you looked like, but I knew you were out there. I felt it. I felt you. My mate." He smoothed his hand up and down my thigh, and I felt my body heat even more, my arousal climbing. "What's going on is I'm going to be with you. You're going to be with me. And it's going to be everything we've ever fucking wanted in this life."

And then he reached out and cupped the sides of my face, pulled me in close, and kissed me. God, it was absolute perfection, and there was no way I was ever leaving his side.

Chapter Eight

Cason

Shit, this was actually happening, and at warp speed. She wasn't going to stop this, hungry for me the same way I was for her.

And I'd give her everything she needed, everything she wanted.

I knew I wouldn't be able to control my bear. He wanted out.

"Mena, baby, my bear wants to be with you, sample you." Those words were nothing but this distorted growl that left my lips, my bear right there at the surface, the threat of shifting very real. I had my hands on her cheeks, holding her face, wanting to devour her.

My nails were turning into claws, my body getting bigger with an impending shift.

"I know this is fast, but fuck, Mena, I can't control myself. I need you like I need to breathe." I moved a step closer and growled low, opening my mouth slightly so she could see my canines. "Do you know what it means when I say you're mine?"

She nodded slowly, licked her lips, and I saw her pupils dilate. She said she knew, but I doubted she comprehended the extent of how far I'd go to make her mine… to keep her as mine.

"I'd kill anyone who hurt you, betrayed you, hell, even fucking looked at you the wrong way." She gasped slightly and I wanted to take that air into my lungs, live off of it.

I was so fucking feral right now that I was being an obscene bastard as I reached out and took her hand in mine. I stared into her eyes as I led it down so it rested right over my denim-clad dick. My erection was a force to be reckoned with right now, hard and thick, demanding to be free.

"But you want that, don't you? You want me to be so fucking obsessive I'd kill someone if they tried to take you from me."

She didn't answer right away, but she didn't

need to say the words. I could smell that affirmation as clear as day.

"Ask me what I want."

She sucked in a breath. "What do you want?" It was nothing but a whisper.

"I want you naked on my bed, spread for me, your pussy dripping wet for my cock." I leaned in close and pressed my lips against hers, not stopping myself, not giving a fuck how fast this might seem.

It felt right.

I felt my erection jerk behind my jeans.

"I—I've never done this. I've never done anything like this," she murmured quietly, and I wanted to swallow the confession whole, take it into my body and keep it forever.

I pushed back and stood before reaching out and helping her do the same. I pulled her forward, wrapped my arms around her, and she rested her head on my chest as if it was natural. And it was. It felt so fucking good and perfect.

There was no way I wanted to pull away, but I needed to touch her, to kiss her. I leaned in to look in her eyes. "I've claimed you, Mena. Do you know what that means to a male like me, to shifters like us?"

She stared at me with wide eyes.

"It means you're mine," I said low, not trying to be demanding, but also showing her, telling her there was no way I'd walk away. "I'll kill any man who thinks they can take you from me. I'll break bones, rip limbs apart... snuff out a life as easily as if it were a flame on a candle." I made this low, deep growling noise, and I felt a shiver course through her body.

"That's... intense," she almost moaned, and I closed my eyes at how exquisite it felt to hear that sound.

"It means I won't let you go, Mena. And I know you want me, want this." I didn't phrase it like a question. I inhaled. "In fact, your pussy is wet for me, soaked and ready for my cock."

She gasped.

I felt my animal push and pull for supremacy. My bear came forward, my body growing, my muscles getting larger, no doubt my eyes blacker, my canines becoming longer.

"You see what you do to me?" I leaned another inch, ran the tip of my tongue up her throat, and I knew she closed her eyes because she liked how it felt. The scruff along my cheek moved over her smooth flesh, and the noise she made had the sweetness of her arousal blooming in the air for me.

Not thinking, just needing to feel her, I closed the distance that separated us and kissed her, hard and with as much passion as I felt for her. My grunt of pleasure had her opening her mouth wider for me, and I groaned.

"I need you, Mena. I fucking need you like my animal needs out to extinguish its energy," I murmured against her mouth, grabbed her hair, and tilted her head back. And then I felt her reach down, moving her little palm along the front of my jeans. I nearly snapped right then and there and let my animal out.

When she reached the hard, thick length straining against the denim, an involuntary moan left me. She whimpered in response. I gripped her shoulders and pulled her closer, impossibly so.

She curled her hand around the iron-hard ridge that was secured behind my fly, and a shudder went through my body.

Fuck, I'd never felt anything so good.

"I want you so damn badly, Mena." My hips jerked forward in her grip. I slid one of my hands off her shoulder and made a slow trek down her side to rest it right on top of her thigh. The heat from her touch went straight through my jeans.

I couldn't stop, couldn't control myself anymore.

In the next instant, I had her standing, gripped her thighs, and lifted her easily off the ground. She wrapped her legs around my waist, her arms around my neck, and kissed me like she'd never been kissed before in her life.

And she hadn't.

We were each other's first... everything.

I knew that, and I knew she was inherently aware of that as well.

And then I moved back, my mouth still on hers, my hands cupping her ass. I turned and sat down, bringing her right down with me so she now straddled my waist, our kiss never breaking. Both of my hands were now gripping her hips, and I pressed her down on me at the same time I lifted up and ground my erection against the softness between her thighs.

"Cason, God." She closed her eyes as she ground her pussy on my shaft.

"I want so much more of you, Mena." I started kissing her neck, and she tilted her head to the side, giving me what I wanted. "I want you to let me claim you. I *need* you to tell me you're mine." I licked a path over the shell of her ear, and she moaned for me, a little gasoline on the fire of our passion. "Like that, don't you, baby?" I ran my tongue over the spot again, and she shivered. "I want inside you so badly." I couldn't help but be vulgar, couldn't stop myself from saying those filthy words.

A gasp left her at my blunt statement. And then she ground herself on me. I needed nothing between us... needed my cock inside her. My brain was fuzzy, my animal clouding my human side. I ran my palms over her ass and cupped the mounds, giving them a squeeze.

I roared slowly, low, and moved so she was now on her back, lying down. And when I tore her clothes from her body, her legs spread as she let out a gasp of aroused surprise, and my much bigger body lay between them. She stared at me with wide eyes, but I smelled her desire.

The hardness of my muscles felt incredible against her softness. I was just a man who wanted his female, a bear who wanted his mate. I trailed my lips along the side of her jaw and down to the erogenous spot right below her ear.

"You feel so good beneath me."

"You feel so good on top of me."

I panted. "I can't stop, can't even control myself around you anymore."

"Don't stop, Cason."

I felt how wet she was for me, so ready to take me into her body. Our hips started moving as if they had a mind of their own, rubbing and thrusting against each other, making me hotter with need.

"I can feel your heat. God, it's driving me insane with lust, driving my fucking bear to the edge." My voice was nothing but a distorted growl.

I speared one of my hands into her hair while the other made slow work of moving down her body. When I started moving lower, her body shook with her need.

"Mena. Baby girl. You're shaking, little bear."

"I need you, Cason."

And she'd have every part of me.

My cock could've ripped through my jeans for how badly I wanted her. I moved my callused fingers against her inner thigh. She started moving her hips, as if trying to get closer.

"I'll take care of you, Mena. I'll make you feel so fucking good."

I slipped my hand between her legs and spread

my fingers through her slick heat. "You have no idea how much I want to be inside you, to feel your body gripping me, bringing me closer to the ecstasy I know I can only have with you. Tell me where you want my fingers," I murmured against her lips, my fingers on her pussy, but I need to hear her say the filthy words. I was tormenting both of us with this prolonged pleasure.

She stared at me with wide, almost scared eyes. "I want you to touch my…" She was silent for a second. "I want you to touch my pussy, Cason. I want your fingers deep inside of me."

My whole body shook at those words, at knowing it took great courage for her to say that to me. "God, Mena. You have no idea how turned on I am right now, how you saying that makes me about to fucking come."

She gasped when I ran my tongue along the shell of her ear. When my hand molded between her thighs fully, she arched her back and cried out.

"Fuck. You're so hot and wet." I licked her ear, moved the muscle along the inside of the shell, and a shiver worked through her. "You're so ready for me, aren't you, Mena? Your pretty pussy is soaking wet, primed for my big cock."

Her answer was a moan.

My fingers were calloused from working manual labor, and I slid those roughened fingers along her swollen lower lips, teasing her. A fresh gush of moisture left her, and I bit my lip and tried not to get off right then and there. I needed her bared for me in every possible way.

Placing her hands on my chest, she gave a gentle push, and I reluctantly moved back. She controlled things, even if I wanted to tear the material off her body and have every single inch of her.

Only a second passed between us, and then she was gripping the hem of her shirt and lifting it above her head. Fuck. This was really happening. I was finally going to claim my mate. And then she was completely naked for me and I looked my fill, taking in her curves and creamy skin. The way her nipples were pink and hard made my mouth water.

I wanted more.

I knew right now I probably looked fierce. I felt that way.

"Now you," she whispered, and I growled, my animal right there as I started undressing.

I was so fucking hard. The only way I'd ever even been able to get hard to jerk off before was when I thought about my mate, tried to picture her, imagined being with her in all the ways that mattered.

And the more she stared at me, the way her gaze moved across my tattoos, the way I knew that turned her on, had me getting stiffer.

My body flexed as I moved closer. I reached for her, bringing her body flush with mine and kissing her senseless. Our combined breathing was fast and labored, and I knew I couldn't wait any longer. I gripped her waist and pulled her up so she was straddling my hips now. I knew she could feel the definite outline of my erection pressed incessantly against her, as if it wanted to be let free.

"I'm going to take you on my bed, surrounded by my scent."

"Take me there, Cason. I need you."

I ran my tongue along every square inch of her exposed flesh I could reach. Goose bumps formed on her body, and she gripped onto my shoulders, pulling me closer.

I shifted on my feet, taking a step away so I could move my body lower, sliding a trail of wet kisses along her flesh until I knew my hot breath teased the skin right above her pussy. She stared at me as if riveted to the sight of what I did. I heard her hold her breath as I opened my mouth and moved my tongue closer to the part I knew ached for me. There she lay, completely naked, her legs spread, entirely submitting to me and my bear.

I loved this female from the moment I saw her, and I knew that love would only grow with each passing second.

"*Fuck*," I said on a moan right before I covered her pussy with my mouth. Over and over, I dragged my tongue along her cleft, moving to her clit and circling the engorged bundle of nerves before sliding it down to press against the opening of her body.

She closed her eyes and arched her neck, baring her throat for me as if almost on instinct.

"You taste so fucking good." I couldn't stop myself from grunting out those words against her soaked flesh.

I flattened my tongue and ran it up and down her slit right before suctioning onto her clit and sucking hard. I scented her orgasm approaching, the smell like right before it was about to rain.

Fresh.

Clean.

Freeing.

A powerful orgasm was building inside her. I smelled it. Felt it. I brought her to the precipice and then slowed before it claimed her, wanting to prolong this even though I desperately wanted to feel her go over the edge because of me.

"God. Cason," she moaned. "Please… don't stop."

"Never." When my mouth latched onto her clit again, I started a sensuous rhythmic suctioning.

The fact that she thrashed her head back and forth told me I hit the sweet spot. And when I teased her pussy hole, slowly slipping my tongue inside, that's when she surrendered to me.

I was relentless as I dragged out her pleasure. When the sensations became too much, she tried to push me away, I groaned in disappointment but gave her what she wanted. I'd never push her, never rush her. She controlled me, not the other way around.

In one fluid motion, I stood and kicked off my pants, fully got undressed, because I needed to be with her right here and now.

I stood there, Mena staring at me totally naked, taking in every part of me, and I grew proud and aroused at the scent of her quickening, thickening desire. And when I reached down and grabbed the long, thick jut of my cock in my palm, stroking the fucker and being obscene, I roared internally as her eyes widened and her mouth parted even more.

"Know what I want?"

She lifted her gaze from my dick and stared into my eyes, shaking her head even though I knew she was fully aware of what I desired.

"I want inside of you, Mena. I want to stretch you, claim that virgin cherry, know it'll only ever be mine." I took a step closer to her. "I want to stretch you out, make your pussy form to my shaft only." I was breathing so hard and fast that my chest was rising frantically. "All I can think about is devouring you."

I moved toward her, knowing in this instance I looked very much the animal I housed inside me. My tendons and muscles flexed and bunched as I moved with lethal precision toward my female. And then I didn't stop myself from slipping my hands over her legs, splaying her inner thighs open for me, and I took in how gorgeous her pussy was.

"God, Mena," I breathed and felt my bear start to take control. I knew my pupils were dilated with lust. "Do you know how much I want you?" I didn't wait for her to respond as I took hold of my thick and long shaft once more, stroking it a few times, because I couldn't stop myself, working myself up even more. She was panting as I brought the crown to the entrance of her body. "Watch, baby."

The air sawed in and out of her as she watched what I was doing.

"I want you so fucking badly I can't see straight, can't even think." I felt primal in this moment. "This is it. You're fucking mine."

Chapter Nine

Cason

The wet, hot flesh of Mena's pussy sucked at the head of my cock. I gritted my teeth as I fed her more of my dick. She felt so fucking good that I knew I wouldn't last.

"My first," I gritted out. I wasn't ashamed to admit I was a virgin, because I'd waited my entire life for her, for this moment.

Her eyes widened.

"That's right, little bear," I confirmed and pushed more of my cock into her. "You're my first. You're my last." I was breathing hard, trying to suck air into my lungs. "There will never be anyone else for me. Never."

When I looked at her, an expression of uninhibited desire was reflected back at me even through her discomfort. It was like learning I was a virgin too took most of the pain of her own virginity away. My mate, my female.

She stared at me with glossy, aroused-looking eyes, her hair tousled, and her mouth this lush, strawberry color.

I snapped my jaw closed after the bear in me roared out in triumph. I was finally having her. I'd finally give her my mark, one where everyone would know she was mine.

"That's it, baby. Take all of me." Breathing out the words, I continued to shove my shaft into her until I felt my balls brushing against the curve of her ass, sucking in a breath through my teeth at another squeeze of her inner muscles on my cock. I gripped her waist tighter, digging my claws into her supple, soft flesh. "You're so hot and tight." I could smell her sweet arousal and hear the little sounds of need she made. "I'm going to take care of you forever, baby girl. I'm going to make you feel so fucking good."

"Yes," she groaned.

Bracing my knees apart caused her thighs to widen far. I pulled out slowly, feeling every ripple of her body contracting around me, and staring down at the tip of my dick lodged at her entry.

The restraint it was taking me to go slowly, to give her time to adjust to my penetration, was enough to make me go fucking mad. I was already partially shifted, trying to stay calm, stay human.

"Cason."

I loved hearing her moan my name.

When I felt her pussy become wetter, more responsive, clenching around my length, I picked up my speed. My strokes were languid at first, but as I stared down at where we were connected, her thighs splayed open, I felt my control leave. I fucked her faster and harder.

Her breasts were beautiful, full, and tipped with rose-colored nipples. The tissue was tight, pointing straight up as if seeking my touch. I wanted to draw them into my mouth, suck on them until she came from the act alone. My imagination spurred me on, and I found myself pushing into her with faster, harder strokes. She didn't tell me to stop. Instead, she urged me to give her more. Her breasts swayed with my thrusting, and her creamy skin became flushed. Already, her eyes were at half-mast.

"Mena," I growled her name. "Watch me as I take you."

When she opened her eyes and looked at me, I rewarded her and myself by fucking her harder, claiming her more powerfully.

"Touch yourself for me." I wanted to see her get even more pleasure.

My mate.

So fucking beautiful.

I knew this was all new to her, but Mena brought her hands up to cup her breasts.

Fuck.

"Yeah, that's right, baby."

"Oh, God." She opened her mouth and moaned. "I'm… going…" She closed her eyes. "I'm going to come soon."

"Give it to me, Mena."

"*Yes,*" she moaned and cupped her tits harder, rubbing her fingers over the tight nipples.

"I'm so close, baby." I needed to hear her cry out my name, needed to feel her pussy clench around me hard, almost painfully, milking my shaft until I came inside her. Throwing my hips at her harder, faster, the wet, almost erotic and sloppy sounds of fucking her filled my head. Sweat made a slow trickle down my spine, down my temples. I slid my hand down her belly, over her curved hips, and ran my thumb along her swollen clit. Just that small touch had her back arching and her thighs clamping tightly around me as she came for me.

"Oh, God!"

I didn't relent on rubbing her clit or pumping my cock into her. Her tender flesh rippled around my length, squeezing me, milking me. A groan ripped from me as my orgasm approached.

"Fuck. Mena!" I roared out. I rubbed her clit faster, adding a little more pressure as I pumped my cock into her once, twice, and stilled on the third stroke. "Dammit." My voice was hoarse, my bear right on the edge, right at the surface. "*Christ.*" I came so hard I couldn't breathe, couldn't think. I couldn't even see.

My canines elongated even farther, and I pulled back to stare at the column of her neck, followed the path to her shoulder, and felt my mouth water. "I need to mark you, Mena baby. I need that wound on you, those puncture marks so I can see it and know you're mine." I looked into her face. "So every fucking male knows you're mine and stays away or they'll be met with my wrath."

She looked at me with big, blue eyes, licked her lips, and nodded. "Give it to me, Cason. I've never needed anything like I need your mark."

My bear really broke free then. My body got

bigger, my form wavering as I lost it. I leaned forward to claim my female. I opened my mouth wide, saliva pooling on my tongue and teeth as I stared at her alabaster skin. I pierced her shoulder, let my saliva mix with her blood, go into her veins. I heard her gasp, felt her dig her nails into my arms, pulling me closer. With my mouth still at her throat, I thrust in and out of her, growling. Only after I felt her pussy quiver around my shaft once more did I pull back.

I licked the small puncture wounds, tasted the metallic, sweet flavor of her blood coating my tongue. The world around me faded. Her nails still bit into my flesh, causing me to roar in approval.

I pulled back even more as she came once again. I watched her come, watched the eruption of euphoria cover her face. "Fuck. Yes." I hissed those words under my breath, closed my eyes, and heaved in completion as I pumped my cum deep within her. I collapsed on top of her, making sure to brace my weight on my elbows.

Heavy pants came out of her and coasted against my neck.

"Damn, Mena. Fuck."

"God. That was... Cason."

Yeah, it sure as fuck was.

Kissing her temple, I pulled out of her with a groan of disappointment. I wanted to be inside her all night long.

I leaned back and enjoyed the sight of her lying there. She was in the center of my bed, her glorious nude body flushed, dots of perspiration covering her curvy form. Her eyes were closed, and I had to control myself not to bury my face between her thighs, lick her pussy until she came all over my mouth.

I could have sat there all night and just stared at her, told her to spread wider for me so I could stare at her pretty cunt, see how wet she still was for me, watch as my seed slipped out of her tight no-longer-virgin hole.

Does she know she could bring me to my very knees? Does Mena know I'll do anything for her?

I moved next to her again, wrapped my arms around her body, and pulled her close. She smelled good, a mixture of her sweet scent and mine. The knowledge I'd given her my mark caused this possessive need in me, this living entity.

I lifted my hand, unable to stop myself from running my fingers over the underside of one of the firm, soft mounds of her breasts. A hum of approval left her; a growl of pleasure came from my chest. My cock was hard and aching to be inside her pussy once more.

She moved closer to me, her ass coming in contact with my dick. She hummed again. "I thought a man only had it in him once. Seems like you're proving everyone wrong."

The way she teased turned me on even more.

Fuck, I'd go all night with her, come over and over again. I had a lifetime worth of orgasms to give her, my balls filled with so much seed that all I wanted to do—all I would do—was pump it into her until she was filled with my cum, until she was pregnant because of it.

I pulled her closer to me, my cock rock-hard, my need insatiable. But right now, I'd let her rest, sleep.

But after she was rested… all bets were off. Her pussy would be sore, swollen, and covered in my cum.

"No going back, little bear. No going back ever. You're mine."

Chapter Ten

Mena

I felt the surge of power move through me, the mark on the side of my neck tingling, an exhilarating sensation consuming every single part of my body.

My cells, DNA, and bones. The very marrow deep inside them.

I looked over at Cason, my mate already shifted into his bear form. His dark eyes watched me, penetrated me, giving me encouragement even though he said nothing, didn't even move. He was patient as he waited for me to do this in my own time. On my own terms.

My hands were shaking, my knees threatening

to give out. I never felt such strength before, my inner animal pushing forward, making herself known, telling me she was going to finally take control for the first time in my life.

But it wouldn't be for the last.

I could practically hear Cason's voice in my head, urging me that I could do this, that I had the strength, the power. I inhaled deeply and exhaled slowly, closing my eyes and finally submitting, surrendering.

I let all my walls and boundaries down, just let my bear rise up, finally push forward, and gain supremacy. The feeling of her, of shifting for the very first time, wasn't painful, but it was a little uncomfortable. The feel of my skin stretching and ripping, of my skin being replaced by fur, of my muscles getting bigger, my bones breaking and realigning... it was all strange and exciting.

But as the discomfort faded, all I felt was pleasure. It wasn't sexual, more like contentment, like I had found exactly what I'd been missing. Letting my bear free, finding my mate. It all felt so... freeing.

And it was when I opened my eyes, looking at my surroundings for the first time as a bear, that I knew nothing else in this world would compare to being in my animal form with my mate. Nothing else would compare until I had my family, my children, this perfect life I'd always had but had never known was mine.

Cason came up to me and started nuzzling my face with his head, the scent of him turning me on. He licked me, his tongue moving along my cheek, dampening my fur, and a low, happy sound left me.

More pleasure slammed into me.

And then he nudged me softly, urging me to go, to run. And I did just that, feeling the ground beneath my paws, the dirt digging under my claws. He was close by, close enough that I knew he'd never leave my side, that he'd never be too far.

And neither would I.

We were made for each other. In all senses of the word.

* * *

Damon

I HAD to get out of there, away from my brothers and their mates, away from the feeling of being an outcast, as if I'd never find what I was missing, as if I'd forever live my life on the outside looking in.

It was this constant hollowness inside me, this hole that would never be filled until I found her.

My mate.

She was out there somewhere, but for all I knew, she could've been on a different continent.

I felt distant, detached. I was getting older, my life continuing to move forward even though I felt like I was being pushed back, further and further until I'd never catch up.

I continued on the trail through the woods that my brothers and myself had made years ago. We didn't need hiking paths, not when our bears trampled through everything. The only thing they were mindful of was being free. But we'd thought of the future, of our mates and children, of family walks and picnics.

And all of my brothers had that now.

All of them but me.

I lifted my hand and rubbed my palm over the center of my chest, right over my heart, right where the hole was, where there was this painful reminder. All I wanted was to find my mate, to feel my happiness. All I wanted was that realization that I wasn't actually alone in life.

I shoved my hands in my pockets, staying in my human form even though my bear wanted out, wanted to run free and get rid of some of this aggression and frustration.

I liked leisurely walking as a human, taking in the sights and smells, feeling the sun warm my skin. It was the little things I appreciated, that I didn't take for granted.

I was at the edge of our property, the lake not too far from where I was right now. The path had since ended, my boots crunching along the rocky, uneven forest terrain.

It was another ten-minute walk before I found myself getting closer to the lake. I inhaled deeply, smelling the scent of the fish in the water, the birds up in the trees.

I heard the sound of a masculine voice, of water splashing. I didn't know why I followed that noise, stopped and looked at where I saw the man wading in the water. The man was facing off to the side, an area where the trees obscured my view. He was laughing, splashing water in that direction. I moved to the side so I could get a better look at who he spoke to, not sure why I gave a fuck.

I should've kept walking, minded my own business. But the first thing I saw was the fall of damp, long dark hair. The first thing I felt was how my heart lurched in my chest when she turned around and started swimming toward the shore, laughing as the man continued to splash her.

The sound of her voice was the sweetest thing I'd ever heard.

And when she climbed out of the lake, the water dripping down her lean yet curvy body, I felt my cock instantly harden. It pressed against the fly of my jeans, demanding to get out. My canines lengthened, my nails turning into claws. My grizzly pushed forward, my skin stretching, my muscles thickening.

My mate.

Mine.

She was there, just down on the bank, close enough that I could smell the scent of lemons and gardenia surrounding her. Everything happened in slow motion, time standing still as everything fell into place.

The man crawled out of the lake, his focus trained on her. I inhaled deeply, the wind coming up from the water. A low growl left me. I smelled desire from him. For her.

But from her... from her, I only scented distance. Good, she didn't want him. If she had, that would cause complications. Hell, him wanting her already caused problems.

And then as I watched him reach out, trying to push a strand of hair off her shoulder, every territorial and possessive instinct in my body rose up. I was jealous, fierce in that moment. No other male would touch her. No other male would even think about having her.

She was mine.

And that's all I thought about as I charged forward, about to make my claim known.

Epilogue One

Mena

One year later

"You ready for all this?" Bethany, Zakari's mate, said and stepped up behind me, smiling, the genuine happiness that came from her making me feel relaxed.

The mirror in front of me was full length, and as I stared at myself, at my reflection of the woman in this white wedding dress, flowers in my hair, my cheeks pink with my glow of happiness, I couldn't help but smile.

I was getting married to my mate, actually about to tie the knot with a big, bad bear shifter.

Nothing had felt more right, nothing as good as when I had first found my mate.

"Ready?" I whispered to myself. I wiped a stray tear out from under my eye and thought to myself that I was finally finding my happily ever after.

My heart was thundering a mile a minute, sweat beading between my breasts, down my spine. My hands were shaking, but I'd never felt better, never felt happier.

I just wanted to make it official with the male I loved. I just wanted to be the wife to this incredible man.

"You're going to do great," India said. "Take a deep breath so you don't pass out, okay?"

I nodded.

I faced the four women. "Thank you for being here for me, for everything."

They all came up to embraced me, giving me words of encouragement, making me feel like I actually belonged.

I took a step back and inhaled deeply. "I'm ready," I whispered, tightened my hold on the small bouquet of wildflowers in my hand, and grinned, turning around. Bethany—Asher's mate, Ainsley— Oli's mate, India, and Maddix's mate, Allison, all stood in front of me, smiling, their happiness increasing mine.

The children ran around, giggling and singing.

I felt tears start to form in my eyes, tears of joy and excitement, of feeling finally complete.

I stepped outside and made my way toward where the wedding was being held, our closest family and friends gathered around our very intimate ceremony, the woods our backdrop, the wildflowers and massive trees picturesque.

I saw Cason standing there, watching me, the love he had for me reflected back tenfold.

I closed my eyes and felt a tear slide down my cheek, laughing softly at how ridiculously happy I was.

The wedding music played and I started making my way toward Cason, my father holding onto my arm, the forest floor beneath my feet my aisle.

When I was in front of Cason, he immediately cupped my cheeks and wiped the tears of joy away.

"I hope these are tears of happiness?"

I nodded and grinned. "Always."

"I love you, little bear." He leaned forward and kissed me softly even though we probably should have waited until our vows were said. The guests chuckled softly.

As we said our vows, the words we'd written for each other from the heart, facing each other, I saw my future staring back at me. Cason grabbed my hand and slipped the ring on it. I cried harder now, my happiness and love for this shifter taking control.

"This is it, my little bear girl." He ran his fingers over the mark on my neck, and I felt it tingle and warm. "Never gonna let you go," he muttered to himself.

"Good," I whispered.

And just like that, my reality was right in my hands.

Epilogue Two

Mena

Eighteen months later

I could see how happy my mother and father were as they grabbed covered dishes off the breakfast island and brought them over to the massive oak table Cason had made just this past summer. It was big enough to seat everybody, my parents, his brothers and their mates, and any future children we'd have. I thought that as I placed a hand on my belly, the growing bump having this flutter of excitement filling me.

I'd gotten pregnant on my honeymoon, something that was special and exciting and had a perpetual grin on my face, because this was our future. The part of our forever.

I looked down at my left hand, at my ring finger. I had to take my wedding ring off given the fact that my fingers were starting to swell, and the truth was I hated not being able to wear it. It didn't matter that I didn't need a ring or piece of paper to know Cason was mine the same as I was his, but I liked the symbolism of it all, loved having the weight on my finger—as well as the mark on my neck—to show everyone that I was taken.

This baby, our baby, growing inside me was altering me, changing us for the better. I felt strong arms wrap around me, sliding over my arms and covering my hands that were on my bump. I rested my head back against Cason's chest, closing my eyes briefly as I just absorbed the love he had for me. I could feel it as if it were a living entity, washing over me, surrounding me. It gave me power, made me relaxed and content, confident in everything that was around me.

Just then, I felt a little kick, a strong push in my belly. Cason chuckled softly and kissed the side of my neck, right over the mark he'd given me. I tilted my head to the side to give him better access, loving his lips on that mark. Hell, who was I kidding? I loved his lips on any part of my body.

"He's feisty tonight, yeah?"

I turned in his arms and rose on my toes to wrap my hands around his neck. He leaned down so he could kiss me back. I needed his mouth on me desperately. But the kiss wasn't anything sexual. It was soft and sweet, showing each other how we felt in a physical manifestation. "I think he's going to be wild like his father," I said against his mouth, grinning, hearing Cason chuckle again.

"You think you're not the wild one, little bear?" He gave me another little peck on my mouth before pulling back and cupping my cheeks in his big palms. He stared down at me, his eyes looking into mine.

"You've got so much fire in you I don't think I can ever keep up." There was an almost astonished, stunned tone to his voice, as if that pleased him. And I knew it did.

"Everyone ready to eat?" Zakari asked and held up two bottles of sparkling wine. Oli held up a bottle of sparkling apple juice for not only me, since I was pregnant, but also for his mate and Asher's mate, who were withchild. Three mates pregnant at the same time. Not sure what the odds of that were, but it was nice going through something like this with others, sharing that experience, our family growing.

Maddix leaned in close and whispered something into his mate's ear, and she leaned even closer and snuggled his neck, a glow surrounding her. I could smell she was fertile, knew they'd be trying for another little one very soon.

We all sat around the table, the champagne and sparkling apple juice being poured. The craftsmanship of the table Cason made was extraordinary, with detailing of grizzly bears etched into the side, even little cubs playing together. There was a forest scene carved into the center. It was glossed over, shellacked so it was smooth, pristine. It had taken him six months to build this table, his free time devoted to this project. And all the while, I'd sit with him in his woodworking shop and talk to him, watch him do his thing, be in his element.

And one day, I'd see our son with him in there, both of them working on a project together, creating something that could be used by our families for generations to come.

I looked over at my mother and father, unable to help but smile at the way they were still so in love, how my father seemed more at home in these woods, surrounded by nature, than I'd ever seen him. In fact, my parents were even talking about building a small cabin right outside of town, this little lot of acreage that would allow him to really connect with his shifter side. And I was actually surprised my mother was all for it, that she admitted she loved seeing my father seem so young, so excited about the possibility of things to come.

I wanted all of that for them. I wanted all of that for me as well.

For me and Cason.

As I sat there eating with my family, with the family I never knew I had but had always dreamed off deep down in my soul, I couldn't help but place my hand on my belly and feel my son kick. Cason's hand was instantly right over mine, his strength and love for me seeping right down to my very marrow.

I finally belonged.

I finally found the purpose in my life, and that was to be a mate to the shifter right beside me, to be a mother to his children, and to share my life with him until there was no more life to share.

Epilogue Three

Mena

Ten years later

"Alex, go get your sister, okay?" I called out from the kitchen and looked over my shoulder to see Alex running out the front door toward the swing set, where I could see Lily going down the slide. The kids might be ten already, and the swing set might be a little too small for them now, but they refused to let Cason tear it down.

Ten years ago, I had a little boy and little girl. Fraternal twins. Lily had been a surprise, so hidden behind her brother that even the ultrasound tech hadn't seen her. Hell, Alex's scent had been so strong that not even Cason had been able to smell her.

She was our little surprise—"double the trouble," we both said about them.

Fiercely different in their own rights, one thing was for certain—Alex was a big brother in all senses of the word. Protective and loyal, caring and gentle.

But Lily was a spitfire, not taking shit from anyone, least of all a bully at school. She'd given the little shit a bloody nose when he pulled on her pigtails. And when Alex found out... he'd given him another bloody nose.

I didn't condone violence from my children, but defending themselves and protecting each other was a whole other ballgame.

I wiped my hands on the dishrag and turned to watch them. Alex was watching her go down the slide, Lily's giggle clear and excited. Cason was just a few feet away, working on a bench for my garden.

The kids came running in, and I gestured for them to go to the bathroom to wash their hands before dinner. Cason walked in a few moments later, sweat glistening on his massive body, my heart thundering with arousal. Even all these years later, he made me feel weak in the knees, gave me butterflies in my belly, and I felt myself falling in love with him all over again.

He grinned slowly and gave me a wink, but before he could turn and go get cleaned up, I reached out and took his hand, pulling him toward me. He let out a low growl and pushed my body up against the sink with his, the feel of his erection forming making a small gasp leave me.

"You're insatiable."

He growled again, his bear right there, ready to take me, to claim his mate.

My animal rose up as well, clawing to get out, to be with her other half.

"Only for you, little bear." He ran his canines over the mark on the side of my throat, and I closed my eyes and groaned. "I'll only ever be insatiable for my fated mate."

Just then, Alex and Lily came running in, and Cason made a sound of disappointment before chuckling when he heard the kids gagging at seeing our PDA.

"Gross, Mama," Lily said.

"Yeah, nasty," Alexa added.

"You two just wait until you find your mates," I told them, and instantly Cason made a deep, disapproving sound.

"My baby girl isn't ever going to be around a male."

I rolled my eyes.

"Yeah, no one will be good enough," Alex inserted, and I couldn't help but feel my heart melt at how protective my two boys were over my baby girl.

We all sat down at the table, the massive oak one Cason carved so many years ago. And I knew that although ten years had passed since we had our twins, I still wanted more babies. In fact, I was fertile, knew Cason could smell it by the way he watched me, stalked my movements.

He leaned in close, his mouth by my ear, and whispered, "Tonight, mate. Tonight, we put another baby in you."

I turned and looked at him, the kids talking about a movie they'd seen the other day.

"You want that, little bear? You want me to put another baby inside you?"

Chills raced up my arms and legs and I nodded. That's all I could do. That's all I could say.

Because when you found the one person who made you feel like forever was in your life, that happiness and love were never ending, you held onto that and rode the wave.

HE ONLY WANTS
HER

STALK HER

USA TODAY BESTSELLING AUTHOR
JENIKA SNOW

STALK HER

By Jenika Snow

www.JenikaSnow.com

Jenika_Snow@Yahoo.com

Copyright © September 2019 by Jenika Snow

First ebook publication © September 2019 Jenika Snow

Photographer: Reggie Deanching

Cover Model: Ryan Lee Harmon

Cover design by: Lori Jackson

Editor: Kasi Alexander

Content Editor: Kayla Robichaux

As president of The Devil's Right Hand MC, I could get whatever I wanted.

Drugs, women, money, but most of all power.

And it's the latter I was most interested in, most focused on acquiring. Because without that, you're nothing. And in the town of Copperhead, Colorado, I had no problem making people bend to my will.

I ran my club with an iron fist, and what we did wasn't exactly legal, but then again the kind of money we wanted, you didn't get by following the rules.

So back-alley deals, corrupt situations, blackmail, and just being a downright bastard… that's what the MC was known for.

That's what I was known for. Because fear got you what you wanted.

But then *she* came into my life—this sweet, fresh, and pretty young thing working at one of the bars the MC owned. I should've stayed away, should've kept my distance, because she was a liability and a distraction I sure as hell didn't need.

Yet all it took was that one encounter, that one moment for her to cross my path, and I was completely obsessed with her.

I found myself doing anything and everything to get information on her, to find out who she was, where she lived... why she was so far away from home.

So I followed.

But her life wasn't as innocent and vulnerable as she wanted people to think. She had secrets. She had a past. One she was running from.

But I wasn't into a fairytale life or ending. That was never in the cards for me.

Because when it came to her, I knew I'd do anything to make her mine.

Chapter One

Butcher

"Either fucking fold or quit pulling our dicks," I said as I glared at Right Hand, a fellow patch who'd gotten his nickname because he'd nearly lost his damn right hand after he'd been caught fucking his stepbrother's ex-girlfriend. Even though she'd been an ex, apparently said stepbrother still had a hard-on for her and went after Right Hand with a butcher knife. He nearly took the fucking hand right off like he was trimming meat for Sunday dinner.

Besides, the nickname fit with him being a member of the MC and all. Now, Right Hand had a gnarly scar around his wrist, and a sweet-ass biker name to go along with it. Guess things worked out the way they were supposed to.

And you'd think Right Hand would have learned from that mistake, that a life lesson like that would have knocked some sense into his crazy ass. But nope. Fucker was still sleeping with said step-brother's ex on occasion all these years later.

Must have been some damn good pussy to risk having a motherfucker come after you with a butcher knife again and go for another part of the body.

"I'm not pulling anyone's dick but my own," Right Hand said and grinned, flashing a silver cap on one of his side teeth.

"I know you don't got anything, asshole. So fold already, so I can go home and crash. I'm fucking beat."

He exhaled and threw down his cards, face-up. The other three guys followed suit.

"Too fucking rich for my broke-ass blood," Boss said.

"I think you bastards like pulling each other's dicks with this pissing contest." Nitro was the next one to speak.

And then there was Scorpion, a patch who I even wondered if he spoke English, given the fact that most of his communication was in grunts and nods.

"That's what I thought," I said and tossed mine down, showing a pair of twos.

"What the hell? You don't even have shit." Right Hand's face was turning a nice shade of red as his anger rose to the surface.

"Had a shit hand… yet here I am, taking all you motherfuckers' money." I grinned and reached for the center of the table, pulling the cash toward me.

"Fuck," Right Hand muttered. "I'm getting drunk and getting laid. Fuck this shit."

The rest of the guys started talking shit.

"Go lick your wounds, you fucking crybabies." I flipped them off and reached for my beer, finishing it off before I left. I had a long-ass day tomorrow, and it wasn't even doing fun shit, just paperwork and legal bullshit for our legit businesses.

We might be outlaws, but hell, we weren't stupid. Having on-the-books businesses kept us on the up-and-up. It made sure we looked like law-abiding citizens, even if we sure as hell weren't.

I was nearly done with my beer—just set down

the bottle on the scarred table—when movement out of the corner of my eye had me turning and looking in the other direction.

She walked out of the back room, carrying a tray. She was tiny as she leaned against the bar and waited as Richie made up her drinks. Her jeans were tight, too tight, because they showed off her slender frame and the way her ass popped out.

It looked juicy... like a fucking peach.

Her cropped top wasn't obscene, didn't show skin, but it was tight enough I could see how small she was all around.

Fuck, I bet my hands would wrap fully around her waist.

She was young, too fucking young to be working in a place like this.

She was too fucking young for me to be looking at her the way I was, thinking about the things I was.

Her long blonde hair was pulled into a ponytail, and the first thing that came to mind was how I wanted those strands wrapped around my hand as I took her from behind while I yanked her head back and bared her throat.

I tracked her movements through the bar as she

set down the orders at different tables. Her cheeks were pink as if she were blushing. Fuck, she was innocent-looking. I didn't stop myself from lowering my gaze to her chest. Her tits were small, maybe not even a handful. But they looked perfect. The little nipples were poking through the material, making my dick instantly hard and press against the zipper of my jeans.

The men who frequented this bar were lowdown criminals, outlaws like myself. They took what they wanted and asked questions after the fact. And a girl like her sure as fuck shouldn't be in a place like this.

I didn't like it.

I called Richie over, the manager of our establishment. He came over with a towel slung over his shoulder, a worried expression on his face. He wasn't like us, like the MC. In fact, he'd been the original owner of the bar before we took over, before we gave him an ultimatum, no choice but to go into business with us.

That's what kind of bastards we were.

"What's up, Butcher?" Richie asked. The older man might not be a criminal like myself, but he sure as fuck wasn't some law-abiding citizen. That's why it made it easy to give him the ultimatum to sell us his bar while we still allowed him to run it.

What could he do? Refuse us and end up in the back-alley dumpster?

Besides, he was good at selling underage customers, also good at selling pussy in the back of the shop during and after business hours.

"Who's the new girl? She barely looks old enough to buy a pack of cigarettes, let alone be serving alcohol."

Richie looked over to where the young blonde was and then glanced back at me. "That's Poppy. New girl. She's been here about a week. Just turned nineteen, I think." The look he gave me was a little bit hesitant. It was the look of a man who thought I said something shady. He knew me well, but fuck, I wasn't some kind of a fucking maniac. "Should I have asked before hiring her?" he asked genuinely.

I shrugged. "I don't give a fuck who you hire, Richie." I looked back at Poppy. "You selling her ass in the back like the others?" He better fucking say he wasn't or I'd break his kneecaps. That thought and certainty filled me so strongly it shocked the hell out of me.

"No." He shook his head adamantly. "She's not

a whore. She just slings drinks and collects a paycheck every other week."

I grunted in response. "Poppy," I said under my breath, instantly liking how it rolled off my tongue.

I could still feel Richie looking at me, but I didn't give a fuck. He wasn't my concern. Now, Poppy... Poppy was definitely my concern.

About the Author

Want more of the Bear Clan? Find them here:

https://amzn.to/2HY5jNF

Want to read more by Jenika Snow? Find all her titles here:

http://jenikasnow.com/bookshelf/

Find the author at:

www.JenikaSnow.com
Jenika_Snow@yahoo.com